Photo: Deb Lewis

Patricia Sykes is a poet and storyteller and is currently a non-performing member of the Women's Circus, Melbourne, for whom she co-edited *Women's Circus: Leaping Off The Edge* (Spinifex Press 1997). She has performed her poems and stories in concert, on radio, in cafés, pubs, libraries, bookshops, festivals and various other venues. One of her poems, 'river salvages', was awarded the FAW John Shaw Neilson Poetry Award for 1996. She lives in the Dandenongs. *wire dancing* is her first collection.

Also by Patricia Sykes
Women's Circus: Leaping off the Edge (co-editor, 1997)

WIRE DANCING

PATRICIA SYKES

Spinifex Press Pty Ltd
504 Queensberry Street
North Melbourne, Vic. 3051
Australia
women@spinifexpress.com.au
http://www.spinifexpress.com.au/~women

Copyright © Patricia Sykes, 1994, 1996, 1997, 1998, 1999
First edition published by Spinifex Press, 1999

All rights reserved. Without limiting the rights under copyright reserved above, no part of this publication may be reproduced, stored in or introduced into a retrieval system, or transmitted, in any form or by any means (electronic, mechanical, photocopying, recording or otherwise), without prior written permission of both the copyright owner and the above publisher of the book.

Copying for educational purposes:
Where copies of part or the whole of the book are made under part VB of the Copyright Act, the law requires that prescribed procedures be followed. For information, contact the Copyright Agency Limited.

Cover design by Deb Snibson, Modern Art Production Group
Edited by Susan Hawthorne
Proofread by Elizabeth Eldridge
Typeset in Adobe Caslon and Charlemagne by Claire Warren
Made and printed in Australia by Australian Print Group

National Library of Australia
Cataloguing-in-Publication data:

CIP
Sykes, Patricia, 1941– .
  Wire dancing.
  ISBN 1 875559 90 6
  I. Title.
A821.3

This project has been assisted by the Commonwealth Government through the Australia Council, its arts funding and advisory body.

for my mother, Jo, who died too young
and for my sisters Elaine, Anni and Robyn

ACKNOWLEDGEMENTS

I would like to thank the editors of the following publications where some of these poems have appeared, sometimes in earlier forms: *Meanjin, Southerly, Westerly, Australian Women's Book Review, Hecate, Poetrix, Woorilla, Women's Circus: Leaping Off The Edge* (Spinifex Press 1997). Some also have been read on Southern FM, 3CR (Writers At Work) and Plains FM New Zealand. An earlier version of 'death, passionfruit & roses' was a finalist in the ANUTECH Poetry Prize 1995. 'river salvages' was awarded the FAW John Shaw Neilson Poetry Award for 1996.

I am grateful to Arts Victoria for the project grant that assisted this work. I would also particularly like to thank the Performing Arts Museum. Its circus archives and the help of Elizabeth Bernard, its Research Service Co-ordinator, were invaluable. I continue to be grateful to the Women's Circus for its inspiration and for access to its resources and documentation, and to the friends and circus women who provided road support, especially Adrienne Liebmann, Deb Lewis, Jean Taylor, Louise Radcliffe-Smith, Jocelyn Aytan, Lola McHarg, Gil di Stefano and Morgon Blackrose. Special thanks to my publishers Susan Hawthorne and Renate Klein, and to Maralann Damiano, Nikki Anderson, Michelle Freeman, Petrina Smith and Jo O'Brien of Spinifex Press for their various contributions, and never least to Claire Warren for her typesetting.

Quotations from *Haxby's Circus* by Katherine Susannah Prichard are courtesy of Curtis Brown (Aust) Pty Ltd.

Every effort has been made to contact copyright holders of material used to contextualise some of the poems. The publisher would be happy to hear from any not acknowledged or acknowledged incorrectly.

CONTENTS

food for the road — 1

PAST LIVES — 5

audition — 7
gathering decor for the merry-go-round — 8
changeling — 9
fishing the sea — 11
nights without sleeping bag — 14
death, passionfruit & roses — 16
divorce al fresco — 18
bread & honey — 19
legend as tourist attraction — 22
changing the medication — 24
on leaving a sister's house — 27
narratives of a household rose — 29

CIRCUS BEASTS 37

iron 39
Opal's cow 41
wolf dam 44
paddock bull 46
catcher 48
working the cats 50
killing the galah 54
laundry animal 55
mutton bird new year's eve 57
blood and kittens 60

FIRE FRONTS 63

legend 65
'the goddess head' 66
Medusa's lilies 67
improvisation no. 1 69
burning off with Joan of Arc 71
contrary mary 76
improvisation no. 2 77
the Firehair songs 78
the hand-me-down-secrets of a red skirt 81
improvisation no. 3 83
living in the palace of the queen of heaven 85

INDIGENOUS ACTS 93

ropes 2 — 95
taking you to the circus — 96
the genocides in marmalade — 100
eating tiger country — 102
choosing lettuce — 106
travels with boabs — 109
reconciliation — 113
Erzulie in the basil pot — 114
river salvages — 117

FEET ON THE GROUND 123

a cappella — 125
this noise — 126
cure — 127
ancestries — 129
north coast mulberries — 131
game of balance — 134
off-cuts — 135
performing the belly — 137
road poem — 139
stories — 141
box office — 144
midnight on the tree of magnolia candles — 148

food for the road

the theories of twist
the turning shifts
of a wire dance

how they walk the torsion
like a spinal column stretches
the limits of sinew

the reach of ancestry
the cinemascopes of hope

★

how much can she carry?
what should she pack?

the wolf spider's silk bag
has the gift of it

all those eggs slung in one sac

what woman to save
herself a prolapse
would not exchange
two legs for eight?

it's the weight
of the choice
all that living
all those circus tricks

how can she lay
any one of them aside?
she is all or none

accumulation means nothing
if it cannot bear its risks

*

change is the rate
at which she travels

all winter she excavates
using mist as reason
to journey the swag

her silk flag's yellow fires
its narcotic pollens

refuse to stay behind
as if otherwise
she might fly conscripted lives

*

every journey
needs its bawd

her yeasty fingers
her gleaming butters

turn pitchforks
to the useful science
of fire toast

the fool is her cure
circus is her cryptic

out of the melting pot
Pandora parades
all things to glory

★

the circus maximus
flooded its colosseum
to stage naval battles

the heart needs
more than shoelaces
to make it watertight
against history's S bends

she's aiming for the last day

when only gypsies
and cockroaches
are left to walk the earth

singing like an insect
dining like a gourmet

on thesauruses
from A to Z they name
and misname her

in Rome
all actors were slaves

this far south
the noisy heartbeats
of a wire dance

acquit her
for at least not mouthing
the word *free*

PAST LIVES

audition

no words come to play
on the grass of no distinction
not one comes forward
to speak its name
to say what why or how
or even to say because
and all the while the sun
watches and waits
like a broody hen
and the lilac anchoring the gate
watches and listens
imperative as an audience
until the child breaks cover
stands directly underneath
to cast no shadow pretend
no drama except her own
holds out one hand two
opens mouth to show teeth
yes and a great swallow
the words can disappear into
can hide in can erupt from
fierce as spat seeds
to ripen on their backs
and outstare the circle
of empty chairs.

gathering decor for the merry-go-round

shells so underside
pink and impossibly
delicate how they can
rough it with the surf
but fall to a collector's joy
the quick ownership
the souvenir death
on edgy mirrors
and tatty box lids
that crosses
some child's equator
as the turquoise voice
the streetwise life
who'd give her
a foretaste of salt water's
sting in the deep gash
its knowledge of tides
its wirewalker's skill
with horizons
who'd be the thorn
in her flesh
and give her this—
that her tongue
releases the sound
a shell makes
when it sings

changeling

you're supposed to be dead
a relic safe between strata
but here you are again
brassier than an icon's
art of reunion
the teacher the cane
the blackboard the chalk
some girl's luscious boy
with fuzz on his lip
a soprano in his throat
the klaxons of power
overtaking his tongue

*

she's born with eyes like cameras
when they worship you
I know she's a changeling

I shut her away
between the covers of her book

a home-made biography of cut and paste
a rescue in the absence of angels

around us street lights stand up
and sing for auld lang syne

you'd woo her with sentimentals
but you've reckoned without the hag
the fighter with the hooked nose

she turns octopus
in the way eight arms
can embrace or strangle
nurture or mercy kill

she'll dedicate to you
she'll take centuries
however long a hero
takes operatically to die

fishing the sea

1 oysters

the day you returned
a carnivore
is water marked
on the door frame

a growth spurt indelible
as your carpenter's pencil

there has been some advance
a naming at least

you as house god
home with his catch
slicked with fish brines
and motor bike fumes

performing
the oyster death
in a small kitchen

or was it just
your pale child's horrors
you holding
the doorway's throat open
as if the sea had given
you a cave's jaw?

doing it by kerosene lamp
a slow wave swallow
the flickering gullet
of a man's right to his own

2 rock fishing

fish dying
in your tackle bag

the ocean's voice
keeping me in line
fiercer even than yours
and prettier

all those refractions of light
glittering like eyes
missing nothing

a lesson stronger
than circus horses
a new whip hand

I've inherited
your flourishes

your backyard googly
could take the head
off a thistle

the cancer
that whipped you to death
had no such finesse

its effects
were all decayingly human

now I've turned grave robber
to give you water burial

a rare tidal peace

you will not drown
the sea has arms
for her own

nights without sleeping bag

admiration or the knife
which is the weapon?

rejection or the hamper
which is the gift?

the riddle's no language picnic
more like a beauty myth

that refuses to be worn
in comfort or in warmth

and so you come to this room
as you would come to begin a life

shocked at the sudden air
and the huge expectant space

enlarged around a heart
fearless as an organ
who lets in her age

with sag in the flesh
with loose in the skin

a no-zip opening
into body unsanctified

enter at your own risk
or think of her

as music in the cupboard
as collateral in the bed

death, passionfruit & roses
(for M. something like an epitaph)

would death have got you going
with its post mortem joke?

its flaunting of passionate fruit
at your feet?   purples

not to your taste
& never your choice
for a wake

I bear them home
to the knife & the plate

to a slice of truth
through the navel

★

yellow bloods sun's blood
that heat you loved

loaded with seeds
to match the feast of rogue cells
that devoured your lungs

their fictions their facts
how they remember us

the surprise once of finding
you foetally asleep
in my car   your refuge

from a saturday night's
punch-drunk fists

decoying the neighbours
with your kempt garden

its harmonious faces
its impeccable paths

*

fear & survival—
your most constant roses

their arbors their arches
their weeping trees

& your gusto shovel
digging annual uproots
& replants

out of hate for thorns
out of need for lives

that pleasured you
better than sex

roses for a bridal
roses for a death

some passions keep faith

divorce al fresco

so are we here to find
an end to begin again
I listen to your mouth
watch for a clue among
your voices but nothing
separates nothing comes
free   the bundle
of papers between us
crackles like leaves
an old story a seasonal
complaint   I watch
the woman at the far table
who uses her spoon
like a shovel whole piles gone
in a bite an immense dispatch
but there's nothing
to copy she's an original
she does this it seems
every day of her life
this art of huge disposal
no beginning no end
just repetition the efficiency
of a pattern that knows
what it knows that disdains
what it cannot consume

bread & honey

remember the bedrooms:
    wake-up arenas
    our gums breaking
    into teeth
    on the cot rails
    the paint flaking lead
    into our bloods
    —how we sucked
    on our poisons—
    while the wind
    swung on the lights
    like an antidote

remember the passages:
    that split our timber
    houses churchwise
    down the middle
    altar rooms offside
    onside one mr one mrs
    one girl one boy litanies
    of his hers a census
    of adoration homes
    growing more nuclear
    by the century

remember the yards:
>& their noisy gravels
>(those good catholics)
>feet & bicycles
>expert at soft shoe
>the liberation pill
>hidden in our purses
>
>ovulation
>by science
>
>evolution
>by laboratory
>
>guinea-pig rats
>dancing freedom's sex
>with our hind legs

remember the roofs:
>nights of corrugated
>iron & moon teeth
>whittling the fat
>from our adolescence
>in rock music speech
>
>*you southern cross*
>*you starry nails*
>*point us an exit*
>*these rooms*
>*have run their course!*

remember the tents:
    life on the road
    our leotards
    full of holes
    a break out
    into leopard spots

    camouflage & rosin
    & a grip like claws

    moveable rooms

    are they better?
    are they worse?

    O wind
    you bread & honey
    you usher
    you torch
    tell any audience
    we're appetites
    who pitch canvas
    in the dark

legend as tourist attraction

(O my rosy O . . .)

sun rise or set?
the forest can't pinpoint
her coordinates

toll roads keep cutting in
with tricky coin   flash
blindness with a message

no pay no play
the economy of slick

should she play lipstick
let the dollars tart her up
as tourist attraction?

a glossy brochure deal
hot from her own pulp
a value added salvation

(O my rosy O . . .)

how to distinguish
her own dementia
from the woman
face down in the creek

who came back
hand in hand
with schizophrenia

thinking sanity
was where she left it

there's police tape
around the body
a faith in clues

the madwoman's bones
are in the last riddling throes
of millennium   *who am I
if not you?*

the forest also
as family tree

(O my rosy O . . .)

trapezing her torch song
at cockatoo pitch

a cremation of sorts
a hymn of roots

*who are we
if not yours?*

changing the medication

someone is saying
(someone always is saying)
there's a new fix out there
some trumpet blowing late
onset delusions some volcano
playing with fire
learn the skills of a pelican's
catch as catch can
its gulpings more salt
than it can chew
but observe its drainage
clever reservoir clever sieve
ad infinitum (dead languages
roll off its back like water)
its runnels and funnels digest
a sea beautifully bountiful

this itch can only envy
can only backscratch
between the barnacles
the lifesavers have gone
home with the flags
but to take time out
to sit here on this rock
for a recurring eternal moment
(call it $1/4$ $1/2$ or $3/4$ time
not full that cardsharp
too fond of the ace)
to sit here in the sun beside

the pelican beside the seaside
in sun visors   camouflage
(you understand)
for the grieving heart
with stelazine in one hand
and in the other olanzapine
the new anti-psychotic
reading directions
on how to keep a son
preferably and sanely human
in the face of one sub-horizon
to the next switchfooted
between tightrope and tightrope

(wean your mouth from the nipple
hold it under the tap
of eternal drug-relief
welfare the multinationals
chemical the warfares
of non and survival . . .)

this tide my son refuses
to compete fish by fish
this son I gave my hymen for
is drowning outside my blood
backtracking in a silver taxi
through streets of dark water
keeping his windows shut
against circumlocutions of rain
and the babbling tail lights
of non sequiturs:

seagulls are stealing chips
from English-people-
on-holiday-by-the-seaside
whose summer of solutions
is not to stop their post-luncheon
handfeeding (but our birds—O
so irresistibly cute when they
let you think you have over them
the power of food) no not to stop
but to kill more eggs

to stop this tide my son
would mean diving
the fallopian tubes and wringing
the possible neck of a pelican
become instead his beached whale
let him fiesta me
with ramblings and seaweed
in the end all water returns home
and the scorpion sings as it stings
live me anyway I'm what you have

on leaving a sister's house
(for Anni)

we're perfecting our skills
of arrival and goodbye
2000 kilometres reduced
to home ground

we've been working
the dimensions for years

fighting the barbed wires
the bluestone walls
their high impossible bars
their iron orphanages

obstacles make bad husbands
we refuse to be wives

the women of our line
rattle their deaths
is it reproach? is it regret?

appetite and denial
are our alternative children

choice is only chronic
for the living

how we've practised it
we've grown reptilian
lethal as Cleopatra's asp

old skins old nests
make the heaviest suitcase

*

the transparencies
in our wardrobes
what are they but phases
of old python?

to slip one on again
is to borrow the satin
of an old wisdom

a tightrope solution
for getting over
the worst swamps

watch for me
on the horizon
of your blue tongues

I'll be the lizard
hungriest for news
and lavishings of sun

I'll take food from the hand
but don't offer me crumbs

narratives of a household rose

1 *from the white rose's mouth*
suffer the children to survive
their countries' vase waters

i
the snow whites
the rose pures

inhumanly
angel me

ii
I am used
like holy water
like baptism

the white idea
cannot tolerate
the public sucklings

of mother's milk
nor the young genitals

flowering
their darker secretions

iii
it threatens me
with fire

if I touch myself

when the season
starts blooming roses

iv
these circumcisers who come
to prune me with knives

are as regular as sunrise
my terror makes them strong

I am cut and slashed
to purify a husband
who may want me

v
my small pieces
are less than hors d'oeuvre
for vultures

who'll croon lullabies
over my labia majora
my labia minora
my clitoris?

vi
all my rose is gone
they sew me up
with thorns

how can my body sing
through such a small hole?

vii
they refuse to list me
in the GDP

I am all debit
my lips must tally
their own audit

viii
mother! mother!
you carried white roses
as a bride

how the years
browned them off

she did not intend
a tragedy

2 the red rose's dilemma
a red rose cannot prove herself
on a bed less than white

i
did mary use the veil
or did the veil use mary?

playing mother of god
kept her white intact

took her hymen
straight into motherhood

ii
afterwards was all red

not even clean straw
could keep her pure

the child had to come
out   between her legs

swimming her bodily fluids
her scarlet tides

iii
did jesus
ever reify his birth
under his mother's
bloody pubic crown?

iv
history hands me
needle and thread
to sew up my daughters

so husbands can tear
their way in

v
to sew up my womb
until my daughters
turn to sons

vi
to sew up my eyes
to sew up my mouth
to sew up my ears

but never the vagina
that won't stop singing
life! life! life!

3 the black rose at the cross roads
*show me the fairy tale
and I'll show you the life*

i
call me rickety kate
queen of spades
the wild card

the black panther
never questions
the heart

that beats
under its terrible coat

ii
if you think
I am thorns

a loss of libido

sexless
as a dry plain

then you must
also think

this aged skin
is nothing

but cellophane

iii
unwrap me
rose by rose

I will pierce you
with petals

do not ask me
for evasions

for the seductions
of an unchanging face

plastic surgery
will not cure
the mortalities

of a circus maximus

iv
I was born
breast-stroking
and bald

this child I suckle
continues me

her breath
is sweet rose
and dangerous

she will make life
want her

she will make life
want to try

again

CIRCUS BEASTS

iron
(for J.)

so it was re/definition
you had on your mind
a building of the body
to a trapezist's swing
and grip   blacksmith muscle
for turning anger into sweat
for balking the incest
beast playing cattle dog
at heel who whitehot
and indescribably loyal
as man's best
barked its roundup song
at your ankles

some things refuse
to die   childhood
as miscarriage finally
denying your uterus
a foetus of cure
as if it could not bear
any risk of repeat

your ghost train then
as a deadly rails
we could not shift
rushing headlong
for your kiss

not the same old
circus racketing
through your blood
but a performance
of iron rocking
into your arms
O baby baby
hush-a-bye
lullaby   a cradle
at killing speeds
that understood

Opal's cow

There are calf tracks by our front door.
Elizabeth Barrett Browning waited yesterday . . .
. . . I think she will grow up to be a lovely cow.
						Opal Whitely[1]
						(Francoise D'Orleans)

Is Opal genuine
or was she Francoise?

tiptoeing among axes
with cream on her tongue

caught conspiring
with a calf   a juicy veal
a literary meat

accusation needs its fat

if she were pork
you'd call the story
a streaky bacon

---

1. Opal Whitely was born just before 1900 and has been described as a child prodigy. The story is that she lost her parents before she was five and was given to to the wife of an Oregon lumberman. The 'poems' I refer to were written when she was five and six. She wrote on any legible surface she could find: butcher's bags, wrapping paper, the backs of envelopes. The controversy about whether she altered her writings when she was a teenager, and whether she was Francoise D'Orleans as she claimed to be, can be found in *opal: the journal of an understanding heart* by Opal Whitely, adapted by Jane Boulton, Pan Macmillan (Aust) Pty Ltd, 1996.

how she supposedly
larded in her teens
to make more prodigious
the poems she wrote
at five and six

pull that teat
and you'll get the hot oil

not from Elizabeth
out among the clover
singing her own cud

not from Opal/Francoise
shovelling dung from the tent

but straight
from the fire's mouth

the flaming hoop
spares no animal

one burnt hair
proves guilt

refusal to jump
proves guilt

an inquisition's
foolproof finale

the encore
the tearing of her
into jigsaw pieces

was it to make
an improbable truth
of a big-eyed daughter
who milked the world
with inks?

wolf dam

how easy to grow fear
in a square of brown water
by giving it wolf teeth
a mother gift to save us
from drowning on a fenceless
poverty farm   her gutturals
convincingly lupine
the panic language
of a near miss

the front windows grew
such huge pre-school eyes
after   *what big eyes*
you have my dear
our new game of fright-fully
imagined hurt   extra fed
by the dog's teeth crunching bone

where to give us outside cover
were the usually ubiquitous
pines? (our soon-to-be school
lookouts for 'cops and robbers')
the windbreaks that still try
to shape the land European
more suitable
for imported beasts

not even the hot burn
of bush fires could banish
the wolf's reeking heat
though the coconut stink
of gorse sizzled for days

how we swung
perilously
on our ropes
those small summers
just far enough above
the gaping mouth

claiming it in the end
as one more scalp
to walk away with
falling into the trap
of an old precedent—
making a species extinct
as a way of putting fear
to death

paddock bull

you might think of grass
summer dry and yellow
of abattoirs and clean steak
of dirt abased with blood
of primary resource politics
spreading its arrival
with cloven-hooved livestock
in a drop of manure
and sweet-breathed calves
across country and culture
their whiffy bellow of cattle yards
annual shortages of pasture
prickling as handfeeds of hay
from the back of a ute

you might smell the cud
and semen of beefy reproduction
cows bailed up for the service
a school yard grown ripe
with scrotum for the annual bull
its fifteen kids taking bets
on the hereford in its home paddock
caught at its hormonal peak
between cloning and a farmer's
pride in his breeding stock
against a skinny kid in a girl's name
a thin shadow obsessed with distances
that dance like horizons

beyond mateship mythologies
so that she almost daydreams
her way around the bull's breath
on a sunshot fence
a barbed wire touch
that takes her past virginal
and orgies of repeat

catcher

she's here nightly
with her catcher's vision
and her front row seat

nothing puts her off
not even the lion's
bored incontinence

she's a seasonal ticket
spider eye spider bait
waiting on tragedy

it will come if it's called
she knows it's a matter
of timing and a trained eye

and who can work it
better than she
with her nocturnally
rehearsed positioning?

when the drop comes
all you catch is the effigy
falling through your grip

the kewpie doll
wearing your face

the too-little too-much
break in the lifeline

one more death
to sawdust

unless you're willing
to pick her up
and take her place

working the cats

I do not like women . . . I prefer lionesses.
The lioness is so much better a mother than most women.
Would she leave her cubs for a damned musician?
          Haxby's Circus, *Katherine Susannah Prichard*

it's talk-back
and the radio claims
he knows a woman
who dances with cats
but it's not his music
that gets you
it's the no-nonsense
pose of the woman
anonymous in white
neck-to-toe frilled
and gracefully ruched
lace so Edwardian
and composed
it pins up her hair
against any stray claw

she could be ringed
by hearth tabbies rather
than the six leopards
eyes obediently front
and sheathed   just fed
perhaps and somnolent
the one at her feet
could be stuffed
at a pinch

a taxidermy fiction
but not the one
above her head
and the two either side
one good bite
if they chose
to exercise
their predatory
and you wonder
if she were there only
for the frame
the instant snapshot
of someone's idea
to pull a crowd
and then fake her
as indisposed
except she without
smelling salts has sat
there long enough
to convince the cats
that she like them
without whip could
take on the crowd

*

solicitude though
how can six leopards
match Mary's 40 cubs
raised to *full-grown
lionhood* and she *one
of the best-natured*

*best-behaved lion
mothers in the Wirth Bros.
Zoo*[1] *who was fasted
each Sunday to prevent
distemper*

the exposures of iron
cage after cage
ample with illusion
spacing their bars
to convince her
not to hide
her young or crush
them for protection
under her body
and not in the last
resort to eat them
to prove herself
the best of mothers

★

and you'd have to cite Mabel
who left her nurse's cap
in 1911 to play
tigers without whip
and gun without
chair and prod
who put her face
in the tiger mouth

---

1. From Wirth's 'Official Souvenir Programme', Victorian Season 1925. Performing Arts Museum collection.

and her body
in roll-over
wrestling bouts
with devotion
to be mauled
and bitten numerously
a disarming
of the sceptics
bent on fidelity
or was it that she
in justice took on
the wild   sixteen
to the cage
to show what cats
in their jungle
had never surrendered

killing the galah

a screech to tear the sky apart
via the head-on conflicts of travel
how these collide at right angles
with wings travelling as the crow flies
how flocks learning to fear the engine
kill thoughts of our being good at scenery
& leaving as we found them the desert's mirages
as if these were not blood but the red wash of sunset
& killing wildlife on the bullbar is not our sport
but how do you not see the landscape
running the other way like an exodus
& the whole stubborn family of galahs
sticking to the bitumen to protect one sick bird
until the instinct of wings makes them desert it
& lifts them above motor heat & the horn blast
that on the edge of a snuff world
thinks it might save something until death
is graphically pink & grey feathers
grabbing a last quick flight on the windscreen
what can you trust if not your own itinerary
relief drivers we drive & are driven
the broken white lines are gaps
& silences in a myth of substance
highway as an inroads a trip metre
the silver city plays no witness
it has burrowed too far in
to want land to close itself off
like wound becomes scar   us too
we're hooked on the bitumen knife
the slash through the heart
that means certain death to flight

laundry animal

i   she's like foot odour
       a refusal to die
       a hybrid Noah overlooked

ii   her lineage could brag
       if it wanted honour
       to the imperials

iii   that gave birth
       to a queen's inheritance
       of wash days

iv   to a lesson in economics
       i.e. gross domestic
       product means

v   whatever the politics
       in crisis the nation
       must have its washing

vi   she's a miracle
       of metamorphosis
       from organic to machine

vii   a No. 7
       a local laundromat
       a *Speed Queen*

viii   classically she's a breakdown
       of modus operandi
       a refusal to coins in the slot

ix   though she's white goods
         enough in clown face
         to keep gods out of the pits

x   (brimstone blackens
         the imperial long suit
         queens have died at the trough)

xi   don't look for her
         among the blue bloods
         the breeding chronicles

xii   track her dungs
         her deliberate honeys
         her sabotage with method

xiii   to the sheets of home
         she's a signature
         to defy bleach

xiv   it was never white roses
         she hates (though give her colour)
         it's the laundries of cover-up

mutton bird new year's eve

two hours to midnight
and the rookery's
an alcohol in the blood
wild dunes wild pulse
the sky a convulsion
of wings a purple vertigo
tunes and trembles
above the sea's cutthroat
edge   adrenalin's

head for heights goes
straight for the thermals
uses wind as tongue
to levitate the bones
she has been reading
a woman who writes
of her own passivity
how she cures it to survive

the Andes and her fatal
tendency to fantasise
how she names over
and over the erotic absence
of *apricots blackcurrants
plums* to keep her veins
alive enough to make
herself a killer of birds

the companion vulture
first   turned nemesis
turned jealous lover
its beak at her infant's throat
then the crippled eagle
morosely dying who comes
alive in her hands
to fight death-by-drowning

in the flight chambers
of the heart it is impossible
to surrender wings
to rigor mortis   to kill
the bird is to be the bird
the blood on its breast
the blood in your hands
the spilled feather

drops adrenalin
down off the heights
leaves vulture and eagle
to soar in their altitudes
like after-image
like circus art

midnight's resuscitation
as *freak show*
as *tattooed lady*
who laughs in your face
she has your measure
your intoxication with heights
your disillusion with falls

her body devotes itself
each muscle flexes
a gaudy aerialist
a song and dance girl
with fruit in her veins
and behind her eyes birds
picking off the years
like calendars

blood and kittens

sometimes I use my creativity
working out a way to kill
>*Alma Hajric, visual artist*
>*from her journal during the siege of Sarajevo*[1]

when your city
bunkers down
under a joke
that makes light
of amputations
you know you are under
siege's dark humour
discovering
as if it were already
a plum in the hand
that the *human body*
is very soft
very unprotected
that your *last battery*
is the spirit
and the brain
that when your heart
craves to survive
you'll promise it anything
life is beautiful
I will bear a child
meanwhile you live

---

1. Based on Alma Hajric's 1992 journals and drawings created during the siege of Sarajevo. A documentary based on these, *Black Kites*, was televised by SBS, 3 March 1998.

an underground journal
in a time without sun
recording images
and words
under *the silence*
the darkness
and the weight
of five blankets
grateful that like
the colour white
you cannot without
water and soap
expose yourself
to the killing test
that buries its dead
in the playgrounds
between the seesaws
and the slides

and so each day
of your cramped basement
you fly the black kites
of art   horrified
by your own talent
to plot death
beyond the fine tip
of a pen or a brush
while the earth
swims away from itself

towards some kind
of oblivion
and revulsion
measures itself
against the innocence
of fur as two kittens
lap at the blood
of two children
freshly killed

FIRE FRONTS

legend

that witch who camped
on the edge of the forest
is gone   her green tent
flaps in the wind
like old years old tongues
about how she hid there after
the house cast her out after
her children grew voices
to accuse her she travelled
the track to and from
like an echidna with
its undersides showing
they say she stopped bathing
when she threw her name away
in the name of honesty
even the fire arrows she liked
to practice with roofs
have run silent
and a good thing too
some say yes a good thing
you mark our words she'll vanish
off the face of the earth
one of these days
her kind always do

'the goddess head'
(after an etching by Elaine d'Esterre)

you're coolly arrogant
among violet dawns

a goddess's luck
this safe return
from the holy wars
against the god woman

you've opened
the navel's viewing room

like sunlight streams
through stained glass

into how art died
under the palette
of something religious

no given name
no patronymic
you're the wild anonymous

the sphinx the artemis
the singing in the blood

it's how I like you
subtle   oceanic

a wine for the eyes
a music for the tongue

Medusa's lilies

they get to you at last
the religious lilies

all those altars
and stinking vase waters
so much proximity

the coldness of their white
and waxy skins   their
pollinating yellow tongues

even death's chilly sex
is not this contagious

so many sacrifices
by candle light
on starched lace cloths

ritual priests devoutly
drunk on blood wines
offering the holy offerings
in the name of . . .

girls chastely drunk
on the heady offering
of their lives
in the name of . . .

the mothers drunk
on their daughters'

pale purity
in the name of . . .

younger sisters
waiting in line
with armfuls of lilies
the radiance
of devotion
heating their faces
in the name of . . .

the generations rising
in roses of smoke
before the icons
in the name of . . .

Medusa with a chronic
cough   offering
alternative lilies
the calyxes of her breasts
in my own name . . .

a true gorgon's vanity:
take me or leave me
I'm no circus costume

owning her tusks
her petrifying eyes
her hairy snakes
would this make us
more terrible
than we are

improvisation no. 1

the theatre arrives
like a calendar

tick off its days
its variable wardrobes

its smoke-fugged
and tireless airports

grab the risk of travelling
between the wars

too many lives
are depleting the ashtrays

*

kindergartens
are pegging their small shadows
to hobble big cat life

in the Bluebeard cells
invisible wives
are cursing like plovers

and if you're looking
for clown alley
it is furthest from the light

*

it is time to exit
the soul's glory box
belly-down among the slugs

tracking their silvers
through the burning dumps
and the runway smogs

honour the gastropods
with sweet lettuce

they are the slow patient ones
the ones holding the curtain ajar

*

you may stay if you wish
and listen to the stage
purring its ovaries

or   your own pickled pair
in the gynaecologist's jar

take them home again
and relish them like grapes

they might burst through
into something brilliant

like spotlight

burning off with Joan of Arc

run mad as often as you chuse
but do not faint
                    Jane Austen

Joan   your old roof
this sky   is running
out of height

arsonists haunt us
like bad weather   neighbours

load each other
with escape routes

we keep tabs
on petrol and matches

every executioner is a flame

*

it has taken years
to scatter your ashes

and still the fuels gather
into pyres

like the leaves and bark
of a culture's hates

*

to torch them
is too much hazard

to water them
takes too much tank

we hoard retardant
and resistant
like rations

*

being prepared
is a brittle house

last year I left you
to burn like an icon
on a doomed wall

you still walk its tightrope
like a woman
who dares infernos

*

and there's this—
two neighbour women
run to earth by a firebug

incendiaries light no torch
for mercy   the same red tongues
that sped your meltdown

consuming the memory
of sky as cool blue honey

the rare things
still going up in flames

★

hour by hour the bulletins
overwhelm with spectaculars

we stay or evacuate
lives burn and burn

the forest fights back
with combustion   a promise
to rise from its own ash

it remembers you
as a hot spot

how once lavishly
you inflamed with the beauty
of 300 dancing girls[1]

---

1. Joan of Arc was once staged by Ringling Bros. *circa* 1913 as a 1200 character spectacle that included 300 'beautiful' dancing girls. Performing Arts Museum collection.

only fools mistake
them for fireflies

an escape night of the senses

watch them work the crowd!
watch them trap arsonists!

*

we stand either end
of the heart's verandah

this was to be the start
of a new extension

a communal raising
after the ash   until Kosovo

killed our hammers (though East Timor
dies closer)   we have stopped

blessing the rain   its puddles
cruel as petrol   pyromania

is alight in them
something newly promethean

raping woman and girl
with the ancient brutalities
of unwanted sperm

*

this new front
how it races uphill

like Tito's
imploded brotherhood

and how NATO calls
on the overworked waters

of humanity
and then answers
with fire power

as if this were not
a thing of home
a thing of warmth

*

it's never the same war
even the phoenix changes

the practice annihilates us
to the torch

you chose to rave not faint

you knew how each time
sacrifice burns skin
it is burning the last house

contrary mary

it takes neither dynamite	*on the contrary*
nor earth quake	*mary's cartwheel overturns*
the business of circus	*the personality*
is its own upheaval	*waters under the rhyme*
in parenthetic intervals	*its cockleshell centuries*
the muscles remember	*to unearth*
the clock as only	*among the soul's acrobatics*
so many years	*a passion for tightrope*
to be had from organzas	*a departure from pretty*
a switch that has a past	*maid dirts when push*
to convince against	*comes to shove*
the speed of time's	*history's full*
war and pornographies	*of x-rateds*
how these like rhymes	*and mary's rudely*
leave scorch holes	*on the wrong side of centenarian*
on a child's body	*like chilli in the mouth*
how she must wean	*is red as a flag*
these off fire	*waving its torch*
in burn-offs	*in a garden's turn*
that take her	*of thirst*
from delicate to waratah	*from water to blood*

improvisation no. 2

you'd call the space
bare   silent
in the meaning of stark

ice-hot as a border crossing
between death
and the imagination

there's no going back
shoes have left
no directions
for a return to feet

her trapeze flies
with the weight of you
in her mouth

you're intoxicated
mewling like a cub
the appalling chance
to open your eyes again
to first light

the Firehair songs[1]

1
she came into the landscape
deficient in melanin
a red temper's deceit
a particular passion
unmarriageably
refusing to smell
like a bottle's
tincture of amber
tincture of violet
her head hair's lustful
her body hair's gross
the sun's on to her
she'll burn she'll fry
she's cauldron born
she's fanatically cursed
she's mud in your eye
a hagiography
a joke in the pub
a heroine so honed
she's danger to the page

2
she came flaunting
the sexual
significance of hair
before abundant

---

1. *Firehair* was a Pioneer Western Romance (Ranger Comics) comic in the late 1940s/early 1950s.

became everything's
excuse for wanting
she was of the money
and they wanted her
the moguls the makers
she was their glamour
their starlet
their scarlet fantasy
a serial excitement
from the groin
of a pen

3
she came
before leather
turned erotic
she was celtic glory
bareback on a horse
she was paddock
turned prairie
she was bracken
made crimson
and waving
like beautiful grass
danger's humiliation
to cowboy fumbles
a girl's own wild
speedy and deathless
they had her
episodically

cornered on the page
trapped in the plot
a white girl
they'd Indianised
with sex's reason
for getting her back

4
she died
under the pen
without innocence
like a war virgin
did they conquer her
at last with the lasso
of sexual revenge
the trussed ankle
the manacled wrist
or did she burn through
to the plotting desk
to the dead wood
like an arrow
flies to the heart

the hand-me-down-secrets of a red skirt

adore my reds
they do not come free

                    sacred prostitute
                    to sex goddess
                    to drag queen
                    to opportunity shop

the cotton field whips
stripping black skins
for my appalling crimsons

                    the family bible
                    numbering its decapitations

rolling heads
in the cottage industry
as easily as beads

                    call me a religion of blades!
                    call me a twirl of bias cuts!
                    call me a sign of the times!

the tiger economies
how long can they
keep a grip on the hems?

                    O I'm dancing I'm dancing!
                    I've cartwheeled
                    with circus beasts
                    across all the continents

how many flags I've flown
in support of ring masters
how many banners I've marched
in protest against them!

                      my gorgeous revolutions!
                      one of my lovers
                      used me to clean
                      his guerilla rifle

when he was killed
I shot the enemy myself

                      who can gainsay
                      a daughter of the cloth?

my mother stitched her finger
to the sewing machine
in the altering of me

                      it's the least of our bloods
                      now she is rheumatic
                      and in need of red flannel

so what if this
is an age of trousers?

                      I've found myself
                      an orphan in a storm

what might she become
with my mouth
around her waist?

                      you are not the first
                      I warn her

                      you are not the first

improvisation no. 3

you were wire dancing
before you knew it

to arrive at her door
her facade's terra cotta

is to improvise
as a life exiting its market forces

★

she's raw this theatre
a flyover
above the history roads

I lie on her boards
to relearn the ecstasy
of breathing

★

it's like prowling the dark
in forgotten coats

I keep getting lost
in the impatience
of the pulse

*

she's frighteningly marvellous
the way she's here   invisibly
in all weather

she's not comatose
a victim of applause
she's a recurring verge

an invitation
to break chain

living in the palace of the queen of heaven

> R. 'Doc' Spalding built a circus on a barge and called it
> 'The Floating Palace'. It opened in 1852 and was an instant
> success, touring the Ohio and Mississippi Rivers annually
> until it burned to the water line in 1865. The acts mentioned
> here were not among its attractions.
> (Source: Performing Arts Museum collection)

1   this boating life
this *rock rock rock*
of glitter water
living its history
of dreams
with $42,000
circa 1850
and a vision
of the standard
42-foot circus ring
afloat **queenly**
on a barge

add multiplications
of 2400 patrons **gorgeously**
backdropped with velvet
lavishly slippered
with thick carpet
and always
touched **masterfully**
with a ticket box
ornately carved

        add a towboat's
        engines to tug
        royally a palace's
        mirrored enchantments
        fire its 200 gas lights
        warm it **charmingly**
        with steam heat
        and **copiously** hide
        the workhorse smells
        in the off-shore
        menagerie

        be the price
        be the ticket
        eternally eternally
        be the year of operations
        that burns like hell
        to the water line

2.   *Ringling Bros. Barnum & Bailey exhibited thirteen Ubangi women during the early 1930s. They were brought out of West Africa by Dr Ludwig Bergonnier. Their 'saucer lips' drew huge crowds.*

                              (Source: Performing Arts Museum collection)

did you think
it was some weird rite

that drew so many
small-lipped faces
through the circus gate

to stare at
your Ubangi beauty?

were willing even
to pay you dividends

for the privilege
of calling you
foul smelling and savage

and to marvel
at your foodish way
with raw fish

and unpeeled
bananas

but not to wonder
at their own decade
how it could pay

so much coin
as if it were a dowry
to the European

who had you brought
out of West Africa
for his enrichment

3.
In his early days as a circus entrepreneur Barnum acquired the 'Feejee Mermaid'. He planted stories, supposedly written by scientists, in newspapers and pamphlets to 'prove' she was authentic and began exhibiting her in 1842 with great financial success.

(Source: Performing Arts Museum collection)

make me spectacular
a *Feejee Mermaid*
cobble me a life
from a dead monkey's
torso and head

and a fish's body
keep the stitches sly
keep the stink low

keep the animals
robed to the profit

liberty and sweet life
a tabloid prayer
of bogus science

and mocked truth
full of gullible
and riches

(don't touch/my
nerve ends [wired
and strange they can't
recognise each other's]
only the breath
that breaks

like a phantom wave
against a seam's
hybrid navel
and calls itself pain)

prove me mute
public me   maul me
keep the dollars chinking
in the tills of heaven

4.   *In this age of ultrarealism the circus is a last frontier.*
           Wirth's circus programme, Melbourne
           season and tour 1940. (Source: Performing
           Arts Museum collection)

the money fats
devoured even Gargantua[1]

Herta[2]
I'm holding you
up to the light

without giving
you a bean

---

1. Gargantua was a 600lb gorilla. Acid was thrown in his face when he was small, giving it a fierce, twisted expression. He was billed as the 'World's Most Terrifying Creature'. A pageant featuring Frank (Bring 'em Back Alive) Buck was created in Gargantua's honour when he was first exhibited in 1938. Performing Arts Museum collection.
2. The Sarrasani Circus offered a prize of 50,000 marks (*circa* 1923) to anyone who could come up with a match for Herta's weight-for-age. She was 15 at the time and weighed 500lbs. Performing Arts Museum collection.

without paying
you a cracker

would you call
this theft?

would you say
it's cashing in

on the freaks'
hall of fame?

your lards
how they'd scatter publics

if you opened your mouth
and let fly with canaries

the show's never over
until the fat lady sings

fly the yellows Herta
don't be a cave bird[3]
for every poking finger

let the owners
keep their poisons

let their patrons
test the mines

---

3. Canaries were traditionally sent into mines to test for poisonous gases. If a canary was overcome it was a sign the mine wasn't safe for humans.

5.   *I'd rather be a racehorse and last a minute*
       than be a plowhorse and last forever
                                           Lillian Leitzel[4]

if you can't kill
the romance use it
adrenalin and rope
at trapeze height
and its half held breath
at Lillian Leitzel risk
willing to semi
dislocate its shoulder
with each spin's eyes
open to the fall
that killed her

her calculated launch
her displacement of bone
and muscle fluid as wind
and deliberately as headlong
a white knuckle glamour
to spotlight the flesh
and make it look easy

---

4. Billed as the 'Star Of The Show' in Ringling Bros. Barnum & Bailey's *The Greatest Show On Earth* (*circa* 1919), Leitzel was famous for her swingovers on a rope twenty feet above ground. With her right hand anchored through a padded loop that was attached to a swivel she would throw her body over and over in a series of flips. Her record was 239. Each time she completed a plange her right shoulder became partly dislocated and snapped back into place. She was killed when her equipment failed during a performance at the Valencia Music Hall in Copenhagen, Denmark, in 1931.

the reaction stretch
is agony   yours
could change place
with hers   the body
can get used to anything
but what will you risk
to keep this grip on hunger?

INDIGENOUS ACTS

ropes 2

upside down you're a
circus gypsy   a wanderer
on a rope who swings
and sings to herself
the way an upturned world
makes the proper sense

taking you to the circus

During a concert at the Gasworks, Albert Park, Victoria, 13 July 1997, Ruby Hunter, Aboriginal singer and songwriter, told how as a child she was taken from her family by white authorities who said they were taking her to the circus.

she's singing for change
on a bare stage
into our bare faces

a song woman
with a voice
and a repertoire
to keep
her throat open

against ships of state
their ten point plans
their next wave uraniums

against empire
from the high seas
selling off land rights
to the holy grab

against fleets
mouthing *'savage savage'*
as a way to takeover

the pearls
playing god
playing circus

>   coming to get her
>   taking her in hand
>   by the hand O she knows
>   she got the clowns
>
>   in whiteface in pompoms
>   creeping their hobbyahs
>   their pratfall etiquettes

★

gloves prevent contamination: poison always travels to the heart (like the arsenics of memory) 'LUCKY KID LUCKY TICKET' when they came she was armed   in black   not satin but skin that live underwear   to last her through the shows   through the sell-offs through the street kid days   through the hazy daze of alcohol   it's a lesson in tracking   it's a lesson in survival it's a lesson in what's culture and what's not

>   these up-front seats
>   this price we pay
>   for 200 years of family history
>   as close as body odour
>   as breath to breath

★

>   her songs of the road
>   reading like advice
>   to the traveller

- travel light
  uncrushables are best

- avoid laundries
  heaping their dark wash behind
  the great dividing dingo fence of race

- avoid soaps anthropologising
  down to the ash for proof primitive

- avoid the starches of assimilation
  'MAKE THEM OVER MAKE THEM LIKE US'

*

native   all of us
who were born here

her black on white move
in language force-fed
by a white lexicon

a music to test
the savagery

playing breast
to our breast

bone to our bone

percussions
to rock the heart

old silt old crocodiles
versus the jackhammers
screwing their agitations

somewhere
between mea culpa
and surface repair

in the end
it's wear the same old roof
or tear the canvas

the ticket and the price
all here in concert
as audience as lyric

choosing colonial turf
or people's land

the genocides in marmalade

these preserving jars panic
at history   sound effects
in glass
too narrow at the neck
to contain the Bosnian
woman's
                  spectacular
her leap for
a food drop reduces
them to fragilities   of sand
she's news
                  they're post-witness
their future considers
its volume against her life running
out
through the holes of a sniper's
bullets   how it pours
like a flagon's blood run
past the UN troops   the city's
bunkers their camouflage
for tracking the war
gratis CNN

safe distance

it's not always greedy
these hectares of bush lemon glut
bring her closer
to the mouth   the marmalade's
fatal eruptions suspect the spoon
how it stands up
in the jam   like a neighbour
masquerading   as cannon

the blood sugars of language
in her living tongue
congealing
in the path of an ant
make *human* more miniscule
than it would like   the season's
batch would doubly bury
her among
rinds and piths   inadequate
breads

eating tiger country

Tiger country is out there . . . beyond the border . . .
    Tiger Country *by Andrea Lemon and Sarah Cathcart*

you were reared on it
it got into your food chain
like a Blake poem

mixed with
the sawdust and dungs
of a Wirth season

piss and saliva
and the terrible fear
that spits from its cage

how this taught you
not to say *feline*
in front of hunters

those nets   tight as noose
on something endangered

*

at every first light
a roaring in the hills
sends guns prowling

for pug marks
for the striped suns
of camouflage

rewards line up in windows
like hitler grants

legends stalk
in whispers and innuendos

the yellow bite
safe at no distance

from the imagination
that traps it

*

the orange dusts of summer
how you breathe them
to stay alive

coating your lungs
with the ferocious coughs
of an animal

driven out
by a farming practice
that uproots its bones

you wash your hair
in its hot ochre smogs
and consider migration

how it brought you
here   to this cull
carnivorous and rare

*

maps are exclusive
to the known

you're stuck with invisibles
the nuances of recognition

smell revives
when the mind goes blank

all that sweat and fur
european as fairy tale
hairy as ogre

exorcism's about getting rid
of the deadly ones

the tiger shoots
the exotic medicines
the trophy walls

*

the tiger won't fight you
none has ever tried
to leap the killing ring

you've stolen her peace
she's no gentle wattle
she wants you off her tongue

she's handing you to country
the cat o' nine couldn't tame

for the blood for the bones for the body

to come home
to land beyond beast

who invites not pursuit
but the absorption
that filters sun lightly

like a tiger going home
crosses borders

choosing lettuce

In November 1994, the Age *carried a photo report on Luzmilla Zevallos, a Peruvian cultivator who, along with nine of her neighbours, buried herself up to her neck in a field of young lettuce, vowing she would die before losing her land.*

*your exposure
as a wake-up call's
morning item
the clotted earth
on your cheek
as the passion
and touch
of live burial
for whose loving
ecstasy is
the conception
of home soil*

*beads of sweat
on a grapefruit
how this can
evoke your skin
its pores those
mouths
wide open
and suffocating
how it can
imagine
a field
of ten heads*

*your naming
of land as flesh
as a ripeness
for the plucking*

*impact as seed
can it reach
deep enough
to touch the brokers
can it get past
that cold kiss
on your neck
speculation's
clever knife
its shifting
of the isobars
to profit versus
lettuce   subsist*

and subside
*how these mean lost
to your two year old
her tears
by your side
watering
the inheritance
you cultivate
her terror
that knows
land answers
according to use*

this position
in a disputed
pelvis   how
holding nothing
back takes
body to its final
succession
its climax crop
this is you
this is us
the same treasure
the same pogrom
dirt   as mother
to the mouth
as daughter
to the hands
as refusal
to come
cheap

travels with boabs

*a boab in transit
under the sky tracks
strung like wire
between gondwana
and australia
by the continental drift
of exotics*

★

rock fall or land slide
there are tremors here

and the settling
of plot lines

she's a dark house
wide as pregnancy's room

for the use of rejection
or forgiveness

★

to get close
is to hear the fruit bats

going noisily delirious
on her night milks

is to measure
the expansions of age

with the ludicrous
limits of an armreach

a thin trunk
cannot hold the half of it

500 years of navigation
and memory   1100 litres
of fibrous reservoir

taking what she needs
from the wind's tongue
storing it for the dry times

she is not alone
most of the world's legs
are out hunting for water

*

so what's in a name?
what's in a clue?

to the guided she says read your page /
for **boab baobab** read dialect Africa /
read two hot continents two hot racisms /
read that in a dry climate the heart
cannot cool itself without the communal travel
of blood / for **bottle tree** read glass read
transparent 'will you be my supermarket
my honey my sauce all my preservatives in one?'
/ for **dead rat tree** read the imported sweet tooth
gnawing at her roots / for **adansonia gregorii** read
dead language / for **gadawon** read mother tongue

*

she's a joke on confetti

what's your language?
what did you marry?

I married books
full of dead trees

the talking heads
the theory wars

the kind of wedlock
that means literate

fictional with gargoyles
of no small dialect

that noise in the head
I go nowhere

without

their weird beauty
their restless variations

*

if I arrive with my cup
she will say don't be fooled
I'm sour gourd

if I go with my children
she will ask what have you taught them

if I go with my ancestry
she will say that's no excuse

if I go naked she will say
yes but where is the rest

*

wheeling as the earth
turns   the boab
throws curves
around the quadrants
can laugh even
at the sun's insatiables
song of medicine
song of shelter
song of food
fierce as a gift
that expects me
to take my share of water

reconciliation

the door opening into the trees
you say is like walking into
a forest whose breakfast
among the quarrels
of rosella and currawong
means sitting down to eat
with hard words
like *territory* and *belonging*
which also means
getting past every country
whose middle name is conflict
afterwards it doesn't matter
that the mosquitoes stab
through each layer
you've surrendered your face
to the white-flowered belly
of a shrub and come out
shining   like new pollen
so that you're more
than a day's food
more than body could expect
to know of lightness

Erzulie[1] in the basil pot

you're my voodoo in a pot
my blessing my curse

I can't get enough of you
sweet and bitter
in bed and kitchen

I'm learning your religion

how the blood of the plant
means death in life
and life in death

*

slavery's still alive
like a bloodhound

though puppified
because you're popular
a delicious culinary

a food's art beyond
the question of race

when the restaurant
means everyone
it's harder to leave

---

1. *Erzulie* is the ambivalent goddess, or *loa*, of love in the Voodoo pantheon of Haiti. Basil is the herb associated with her powers.

when history arrives
with its land order
against appetites

who like your own
mean indigenous

★

possession as $^9/_{10}$ths
of a law   how
this contracts you
to lean treasurings

I keep you potted
out of fear you'll run amok
and expose us

to weed killers
to plant control

forgive the cowardice
I own no property

★

I've heard you
gnash and mourn
as Erzulie Ge-Rouge
when love goes wrong

and I've seen you weep
enough seeds to fruit
companion volatiles

and then bed down
so pungently
you take root

*

Erzulie loa
you're every woman
who cannot return home

the cost is anything
but neutral   this
is no green poultice

you're stuck
with my address
and your teacher's luck

the garden is growing braver
but you'll promise it
no remedy

river salvages

*(a conversation with Connie May Fowler's
River of Hidden Dreams)*

1
you purr through the door
like a great cat   a story tiger
generations of river
ancestors streaming
from your back
*we are the dispossessed
remember us!*

your arrival makes me
a night reader   I take to my bed
as soon as the sun goes down
reconstructing your voice
with the key you planted
under the text to say
nothing that grows flesh is objective
this is a grand-daughter
using no device but her art

page by page your story
pours over the spread
white ancestors
drag yours off in chains
your Seminole grandmothers dance
their rage on my knee caps
such colonials! such bigheads!

your Sadie Hunter
bulges my house
with wet fur
she's rank as sweat
a human animal with claws
a smasher of mirrors
a destroyer of images
of herself her tribe
as celluloid discards
on North America's
cutting-room floor

you think the colonial edit's over?
look around you poor fool
look in your own back yard!

2
this is no cinema
this is the everglades
and love is a dead-end bay
give me my Sparrow my boat
my bird and I'll teach you love
I'll tear your soul out!

tourists line Hunter's rails
with blanched faces
having paid for sensation

she holds them captive
with her slavery tales
she's all cobra all venom

until the worm of civilisation
stares her down

not even the stars can
help her swing counterwise
and vomit the tourists up
for the 'gators   that feast
to ease the tick-tock of her hate

under this cold sky
there must be ice
to cool the gauntlet of the heart!

on dry land
you offer her no hides
only a dying heron
its great blue body
feathering the dust
its yellow eye shocked to death
by a speeding culture
it had no instinct to read

the stones of the road
bleed through her armpits
wing stumps ride escort
on her shoulders
she has flown this cycle
before   how many times
must the sacrificial bird
die in the arms of a character
before we are reborn?

3

in the land of ten thousand islands
lie pools the sun never finds

all your power is in her arms
in those long fingers that tickle
the symbol and float it loose
a tiny coffin bearing a kinglet
north? south? east? west?

Ah Jesus!   another saviour!

all irony depends
on recognition
and isn't it her right
to second-guess the plot
to take the heron's wings
from the freezer
and tie them on with river grass
didn't I keep them just for this?
wings not for flight
but for drowning
to make sure this child
will not rise and rise
in spirals of white
that racial air
that veil

hunter as priestess

I give you death by water a second time
hush! my Sparrow *will sing you to sleep*

it is all the novelist has
this symbolic art this sweet
revenge   this taking
of death from our hands
and plunging us
to an optimistic depth
to breed yet another chance

4
the river tiger prowls its banks
its belly low-slung   puckered
around the red wound
where the knife
tried to cut out its tongue

*steal a people's language
and they forget who they are
leave only one word
and something lives*

like *river*
like *grand-daughter*

fed by ten thousand
umbilicals   islands
of tiger milk

chain breakers

they're all ours now
the ankle shackles

exhibits for our museums
our hoarding houses
our temples of rust

5
Hunter hears stories
breeding again
among the mangroves

enough of them
to give back your pen

she is all pilot
under her
the *Sparrow* rocks
and croons

lifeboat as cradle
river ink as lifeblood
as compass

as tiger

who swims and swims
trailing ripples
of indelible words
by the yellow lamp
of a heron's eye

We're taking back our life
don't think it rests with you!

FEET ON THE GROUND

a cappella

in this room week by week
the walls wait for our feet
our voices the windows look
inwards rather than out
and the door   the door
is ready for entry thinking
we will return will come
back with our hands
and tongues full of music
it has waited year
by year has kept opening
its dream of admittance
loud in its hinges
and now we arrive
not knowing we were
coming back not knowing
we had ever been here
and something is laughing
something is friend
in the voices in the names
and the room settles
endlessly like (of course) sand

this noise

some acts grow overtired
and betray themselves
when the moon is dark
they buy torches
to window sit
against catastrophe
and demand you closer
than the next bed
so that your breath
can punctuate
their night sweats
and order you radiant
against storm and tempest
and hedge you
against cocktails
iced with a snow leopard's
quiet and deathly
stalk   this insistence
to be moonly luminescent
theirs to throw light
like a clear white O
on their incessant quakings
they'd watertight you
like contract
even sue in the end
to stop all
and every travel
that would lose them

cure

in a room whose lingua is silence
        hers is the most
she's lunar and remote
        inside cancer's white
a blank name tag's distance
        between intimacy
and breath

so that when they arrive
        you want to take
the missionary out
        of the singers
fanatically so earnest
        they enthuse
like a rugby scrum's
        passion for the ball
that life leather
        that bounce

and you want to cheer
        her pale obstinacy
how it buries into wall
        like a print's withdrawal
behind glass
        loathes the room it's hung in

    these plums these raspberries
to keep singing
    bowls of fruit
is ridiculously nostalgia
    her retreat is an affair
face-on and twisting
    with the mortality voice
its coded love
    cupped like a lover's hands
on her mastectomy
    the most noise
she can take

ancestries

materialise as dream if they must
it's the one route
you can't shut out or shut up
like this remote bay's flesh
and cliff   blood and water
bone and rock   eloquently
as if access were always open
through memory to wild genes
this shore   curves
like an arm holds you face to face
with your own mutations
wire dances so busy learning
themselves they have forgotten
how to feed

expose stick figures in the sand
flow inside their crumbling edges
like a river like a canal like a vein
all revelation stirs its acids
you'll catch something
procrastination never taught
tightrope to swim

watch the hunger
who swaps land for ocean
do it clothed
as if stopping to undress
might risk the impulse
watch the tethered pelican
strain towards the swimmer
with your own desire

a hard bird to catch
even its feathers
are stripped of muscle
the bill that can inflict
has been robbed of its fluency
it knows it has been
made pitiful   it knows
that I know

to take the thong from its neck
is as easy and hard as balance
the sun tilts the horizon
towards pitiless and glare
you're back-doored and buskerless
wide open to some touch
in waking code you would call
an ecology of will
a wind with a subtle mouth
to lift the hairs on your arms
and give the pelican
back its flight

north coast mulberries

these september hungers

mulberries so ripe
they crave the mouth

blood fruit at blood heat
they come with the job

this minding of a house
annually with doors
that open and shut

on passages so wide
they split the heart

*

each year is greedier
for less distance
less ringbark

the tree worries
about orphans
like a mother
cut down too young

*

the intimacies of the face
how they die in the mask

you've been sucked
through the eye pits
of your own imprint
to the other side
of poinsettia

where being away
means being absent
from the roots

*

Europe squandered you
on cities and facades

workload is shrinking
you towards reticent
and withdrawn

what good is water
in the outdoor bath
if the tongues are gone?

*

my tightrope
has become a towrope
for misadventures

handy you might think
for the battered car

what drives our separation
if not a passion for equal

before man
before god
before each other

game of balance

instructions are	*the game doesn't come*
as absent as technique	*boxed each crossing*
a vertigo for eyes	*has to make*
strung to horizons	*her own rules*
in weather	*for the tightrope*
of their own making	*falling the first victory*
the wire's neuter	*is to know feet*
the doubts	*are not the trip wires*
are all slyly	*it's the eyes can't believe*
intestinal	*the point of balance*
like pockets of gas	*is magnetic rehearsal*
a clumsiness of old acids	*the upside down version*
learning fall by fall	*like monkey like prehensile*
the ways of crossing	*is her best position*
like a clown's	*for laughter*
edit is humour	*a hunger's proof*
without script	*that the ends are tied*
without umbrella	*in a game of balance*

off-cuts

so you have chosen
diamantes & black leather

something brilliant
something cold

something to stand up
to spotlights

& hard wear
something appropriate

to stilts
their steel shins

their glittering silvers

do not expect them
to bend

do not expect them
to bow

they have learnt
to break myth

to see through
butcher shop glass

& its blinding
white trays

into the difference
between lamb's fry

& your own liver
is a practice called offal

& instructions
to saute   delicately

performing the belly

All you got to do if you want to make
the crowd laugh is stick out your belly,
and shake your backside at it.
                Haxby's Circus, *Katherine Susannah Prichard*

the winter of politics
the need of a good laugh
all those cold privatisations
of heat water light   life
by the grace of capital

so shake your backside
at the privateers
they've been rehearsing
takeovers long enough
to have worked up to humour

it's better to be obscene
than depressed
to use the belly
over rhetoric

dice entre las piernas
says the Spanish
she speaks
from between the legs

pissing on politics
that old talent
the genitals of humour
alive under the skirt

cut to Baubo
out on the crossroads
giving Zeus the finger
making her audience laugh

a fire in the belly
rubies in the navel
hot coals hot comedy

snow-job seasons
how they work the flesh

road poem

no revs but the dust
        of a joker's feet in flight
from a walled city
        before the gates lock
& her eggs run out
        the only clowns
left *in*side she says
        are millennium's
& you need
        a credit card for that
from ambition's
        brilliant chandelier
like a roulette of light
        it can't wait
to count down
        to No. 1 again
towards some everest
        as if life's somewhere
else she says
        not here not now
& junk mail's
        all over the street
in a party mood
        with bar codes of opportunity
& the stock market's
        doing dividend drops
down the santa chimney
        like a hallelujah chorus

      & no moon's too high
            for the consumer horse
to jump cart over
            & that she's a skin of wine
& will I join her the ant way
            scavenging so close to the bone
that food salivates
            to be so wanted

stories

(after the reflections of a 110-year-old Welsh woman televised on Angry Earth, SBS, *25 February 1995)*

your last legs
they're so Welsh
throwing off old censorships
the englands the empires
the scold's bridles
remember the stories
and hope blood is
listening in the veins
of a grand-daughter
while life wrinkles
like aged cabbage
because at 110
you are old
and the nursing home
banishes your cases
of personals downstairs
to dark concrete
because they're impediment
to the aged care
that banks its profits
medicine glass by capsule

lay them out as you laid out
your dead husband
and open their bowels
point them like mirrors
at the english soldiers
who raped your genitals
and killed your desire
include the receipts
from the workers' hospital
that failed to exist
and the sanitorium
your doctor placated
with a rich woman

poison and cure
the story's will
its reading at the edge
of the forest pit
where your son
and his gypsy lover
trapped one
of the rapists
then threw life
down to him
in a hessian bag
until he dies
of snakebite

on tv's tourniquet
its constriction
of 110 years
to a few time bytes
you don't care about
only these hours left
to fight dust to dust
by the tongueful
and inherit the ears
of a grand-daughter:
remember the stories Gwen
remember the stories

box office

between two rotting piers
who reach out into the sea
like arms rigid with loss

as if they petrified
in a mad longing
to possess water

trust us we are your eyes

as if their crumbling
feet must live on
among the driven tides

among this woman
reattaching her skin
with sequins

& this man
whose arthritis
uncushions the sand

& this seahorse child
cavorting among the syringes

watching them come
up for air to face
& face the aesthetics
of this beach fix

this strewn foreshore
staring them between the eyes

as a choice

between two plastic bins
one green one brown

  trust us we are your eyes

your gull gatherers
your chameleon sockets
gritty as this sand's melodramas
between the toes

constant as andromedas
pulling your oars of
seaweed & wave towards
some tanker

because oil is a deadly
swimmer & the billboards
are busily with turnover

  trust us we are your eyes

safe as goggles
in the workplaces of change

we'll unhallow for you
bolt by bolt
or sing you tullamarine

riverlike as the traffic
flows under its new pylons
ultra with red ultra with yellow

    p
     h
      e
       n
        o
         m
          e
           n
            o
 l
  o
   g
    i
   c
    a
     l
      l
       y
almost an overhang's threat
at the point of a sword

as if the next millennial clock
plans to start things off
with a sky war

      trust us we are your eyes

the soles of your feet[1]
your circus
for the season

---

1. *The Soles of our Feet* was a circus season on the theme of reconciliation by the Women's Circus, Melbourne, 1998.

via a script
from the crow's nest
of imagination

as if a women's art
has the most to celebrate
the most to revive

in sweating an audience
ashore whose advantage
is not to be vikings
but to have hindsight

> *trust us we are your eyes*

your rejuvenations
of salt water
your legends of belief

though something's up for sale
something wants us gone

to pass us off as fun parks
getting off on terror

we are nothing if not loyal

we can be any demolition's excuse
to make way make room

we can be any view
across the bay

we can be any glass face
between the eye & the sea

midnight on the tree of magnolia candles

midnight is her arrival
as white silence
on a night without luminary

to hear throats cracking
under some foot
to hear chains rattling
in the convict cabins

split seconds
crank a song out of her
like a sad banjo

she wants the normality
of an everday night

the neighbour's dog
coming in to spray
pugnacious urine
on the cat's territorials

the way it takes fright
at the after-image
of a cat's body dancing
in parabolic ecstasy
like a tiger's love of water

not this pale reach
of her candle flowers
that makes every link
in the fence a life gone
too soon

not these faces
coming like shadows lurch
along strung wire
in search of light

    ★

they have come
with their ovulations
to her circus of repair
via the butterfly road

whose dead wings attach
like a second skin   mothers

to a new species
of disappeared
this is flight   the way they spread

    their arms across the yard
    as if they can block the genes
    that put the weed killer in the crop

what is half a season's butterflies?

       more or less
           less or more
       this is a time of disposables
           our wombs are death ovens

       they have always known this

continuity   is the faces strewn like petals in
the night grass
continuity   is the virgin uterus they choose
to future with
continuity   is the hysterectomy who refuses
to be a cure
continuity   is the digging stick and the water bowl
the thesis the microscope
the wandering howl
that crawls from its tent

arriving
in a rented yard
as white holes
in the wind
whose frost
is sometimes
the closest thing
to bread

★

she refuses
to light the barbecue
and burn flesh

but she is nothing
if not communal

she has cleared marriage
out of the house
to make room in the compass

she has grown a resistance

*but she **will***
use the dark fire
the call and response
voice   the edgy
saw that cuts
into the heart
of what perverts
tree to timber
and she'll use the bawd
as the poker tongue
the hot lick
to prod the mind

to the tamed address

for those who come
to dance face-to-face naked
over midnight grass

and bed themselves down
in her translucent cups

she would teach them
as she taught bee and honeyeater
to revive themselves in sips

but how can she choose
a life above a life?

what is your disease?
what is your war?

the compassion trap
the dilemma seed

there are never enough candles
there are never enough cups

urgency's white need
is always afloat
in the yards of the night

no angel's circus no chloroform
she's every tree earning its dirt
among dim stars dim light

and the body
out of their useless
despair you cannot call
her an illusion
she's a true example
of her species'
luminosity
or
an ignis fatuus
to eyes
that would keep
their blinds drawn
while trains stealth past
like stalkers
carrying their nuclears
their secret wastes
towards some innocent dump
—when she bruises
it is purely climatic—
and so far the next hour
is always arriving
as the unknown familiar
the warm breath
of a mammal
rising like pale
unreadable smoke
the ash in the urn
the blood in the wine
the shared bottle
and she'll drink it
in her own kind
like all things deciduous

OTHER POETRY TITLES FROM SPINIFEX PRESS

Susan Hawthorne
Bird

> *Birds don't fly with leads, I said.*
> *Safety belts are to learn with, not to live with—*
> *I'm safer on the trapeze than crossing the road.*
> *And I do that every day, often by myself.*

So thirteen-year-old Avis argues when confronted by the limitations imposed on her at school.

Many-eyed and many-lived is this poet . . . To the classic figures of Sappho and Eurydice she brings all the Now! Here! sense of discovery that fires her modern girl taking lessons in flight. — Judith Rodriguez
ISBN 1 875559 88 4

Louise Crisp
Ruby Camp

Crisp's insights and perceptions are so original and intense that she has needed to find a new language, precise and sensuous, mysterious and revealing, held in a fine balance of rhythm and phrasing. She creates a radically new way of 'knowing' the East Gippsland bush: "*strong as illusion the dream works/ its way into landscape*". It is finally a book about joy. — Marie Tulip

Miriel Lenore
Travelling Alone Together

Three journeys across the Nullarbor and time are interwoven as Lenore explores our myths.

This poet/traveller is incredibly modest and respectful of what is given her to experience. She travels across her many landscapes – naming without appropriating. — Alison Clark
ISBN 1 875559 83 3

Merlinda Bobis
Summer was a Fast Train without Terminals
An epic of the old Philippines, lyric reflections on longing, and an erotic dance drama make up this fine collection.
Bobis can produce some genuinely haunting pieces. This is a touching work from an established poet.
— Hamesh Wyatt, *Otago Daily Times*, NZ
ISBN 1 875559 76 0

Sandy Jeffs
Poems from the Madhouse
This is disturbing but quite wonderful poetry, because of its clarity, its humour, its imagery, and the insights it gives us into being human, being mad, being sane. I read and read — and was profoundly moved. I delighted in it as poetry; I was touched by its honesty, courage and vulnerability. — Anne Deveson
The language challenges her with fifty names for madness, writing of a life of vigilance and struggle, she enlarges our understanding of human capacity. — Judith Rodriguez
Certificate of Commendation, Human Rights Award for Poetry, 1994
Second Prize, Anne Elder FAW Award, 1994

Deborah Staines
Now Millennium
Deborah Staines' respect for and awareness of language's dynamic possibilities bring inner and outer worlds attentively alive.
— Fay Zwicky
This book is really wild . . . There's so much passion and commitment there and she's drunk with words. — Dorothy Hewett
Winner, Mary Gilmore Award, 1994
ISBN 1 875559 20 5

Robyn Rowland
Perverse Serenity
What happens when an Australian feminist falls in love with an Irish monk? Daring, passionate and forceful poetry about the limits of love and obsession.
Here is writing not afraid to be vulnerable, not trapped in literary artifice, not reticent about emotion, its hopes, its fears, its withdrawals and assertions, which we all share and which enrich our humanity.
— Barret Reid
ISBN 1 875559 13 2

Diane Fahey
The Body in Time
Diane Fahey pieces together a world – with integrity and incomparable delicacy – much as the fragile light of a star defines a universe.
— Annie Greet

Jordie Albiston
Nervous Arcs
Jordie Albiston writes with sharp intelligence, lyrical grace, and moral passion. A name to watch for. — Janette Turner Hospital
Winner, Mary Gilmore Award, 1996
Second Prize, Anne Elder FAW Award, 1996
ISBN 1 875559 37 X

*If you would like to know more about Spinifex Press,
write for a free catalogue or visit our Home Page.*

SPINIFEX PRESS
PO Box 212, North Melbourne, Victoria 3051, Australia
http://www.spinifexpress.com.au/~women